BACK IN THE BAY

Philip Bovenkamp

BACK IN THE BAY

© 2010 by Philip Bovenkamp

All rights reserved. No portion of this book may be reproduced in any form without written permission from the author, except for brief excerpts in reviews.

Scripture quotations taken from the New American Standard Bible®, Copyright © 1960, 1962, 1963, 1968, 1971, 1972, 1973, 1975, 1977, 1995 by The Lockman Foundation
Used by permission.

ISBN-13: 978-1-4536-9943-0
ISBN-10: 1-4536-9943-0

Printed in the United States of America

for Jillian

Faithful is He who calls you, and He also will bring it to pass.
−1 Thessalonians 5:24

On the beach at the far end of Finnegan's Bay,
in the evening when people had gone for the day
and all that was left were some gulls on the shore,
the tide reached a level it hadn't before.

It rose right on past the old high-water mark
(and it made me start thinking of building an ark!)
until finally the rise of the tide was complete
and it turned itself 'round and began to retreat.

As the ocean flowed back from that high-water spot,
the water took with it the things it had brought—
from tuna to salmon to slippery eels,
a walrus with tusks and a family of seals . . .

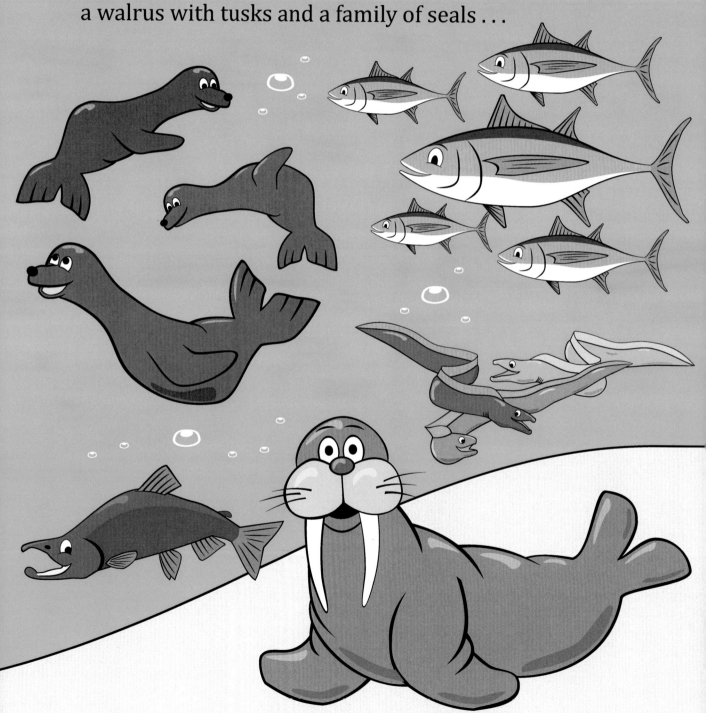

. . . a turtle with barnacles stuck to her shell,

and a lobster or two and a dolphin as well.

The shrimp and the snails were swept swiftly away

and gently set down safely back in the bay.

But not every creature washed back with the tide—
the starfish were left on the sand as it dried.
As far down the beach as a person could spy
were thousands of starfish like stars in the sky.
They were stuck on the beach as the water receded,
and water was one thing those poor starfish needed.

When morning had broken and out came the sun,
those sad little starfish could not walk or run
to escape to the water and out of the heat
because though they have legs, starfish haven't got feet.

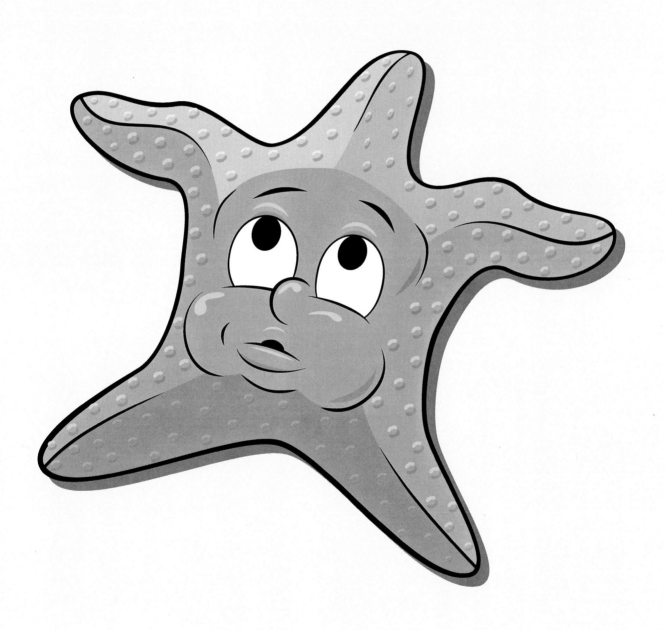

There was one purple starfish much smaller than most,
a starfish named Simon stuck there on the coast.
He wondered what happened or what he'd done wrong,
till a hermit crab happened to bobble along.

"Oh sir," shouted Simon, "a word if I may,
do you think you could help me get back in the bay?"
But the hermit crab grunted and bobbled away.

A big starfish lying nearby in the sand
said, "It's silly to ask a small crab for a hand.
Don't you think he has things more important to do
than to worry about what might happen to you?"

"I suppose that you're right," Simon said with a sigh,
"you're older and that makes you wiser than I."

He slumped on the beach and he started to fret,
but then he thought, *maybe I'm not finished yet,*
because down toward the water from out of the fog
came a little old man who was walking a dog.

When the man saw the starfish spread out on the ground, he shook his head slowly then looked at his hound and said, "Jasper, these starfish won't last through the day if they don't get some help getting back in the bay."

"We're saved," shouted Simon. "This dog and his master have saved us today from impending disaster!"

But the old man continued and said, "It's quite clear
I could never do all of this work in a year.
And besides it's the government's job when we call
to care for the people and starfish and all.
Now I'm a good citizen and a taxpayer,
so when I get home I will write to the mayor."

"The mayor," said Simon, "when he gets that letter,

will send lots of help to make everything better."

The big starfish smirked as he cleared his dry throat.

"I doubt it," he said, "because starfish don't vote."

Soon after the man and his dog went away,

two women in jogging suits jogged by the bay.

When they saw what a fix those poor starfish were in,

one said, "We should help, but where would we begin?"

"We'll form a committee!" the other replied,

"And we'll all get together, and then we'll decide

how to deal with these starfish left here by the tide."

"A committee," said Simon, "sounds like a great way

to help all us starfish get back in the bay."

"But first," said one woman, "there's much we must do—
our group needs a name and a slogan or two,
and we'll hand out some flyers and make a big sign
with pictures of starfish built in the design.
We'll have a fund raiser and membership drive
and do it all so these poor starfish survive."
So it was agreed and away they both ran
(already revising big parts of their plan).

"Do you think," Simon asked, "they'll be back before long?"
The big starfish answered, "I hope that I'm wrong,
but even if they make it back to this shore,
it's liable to take 20 meetings or more.
By then things down here will not be very pretty,
but that's what you get when you have a committee."

Then next down the beach came a man with a book,

who read as he walked without stopping to look

to see where he was stepping or whom he might squish

(like a smaller-than-average-size purple starfish).

"I almost got crushed!" Simon said with emotion,

"but maybe he'll help us get back in the ocean."

When finally the man saw that there on the shore
far away from the water were starfish galore,
he said, "What has happened is perfectly clear—
the bay got too crowded with starfish down here,
so nature stepped in and she kicked out a few
so the ones who were left would have room to make do . . .

. . . Now, in the big picture, it's all for the best

(if not for these here, then at least for the rest).

It's perfectly fair—nature is quite judicious.

This theory is called *The Survival of Fishes*."

"Fair?" shouted Simon. "I must disagree.

Fair would be helping us back in the sea!"

But he started to think it was not meant to be.

The man turned a page and he went on his way
and he almost bumped into a boy by the bay.
The boy said, "Excuse me," and stepped to the side,
but the man just kept walking and never replied.

"If a man and his dog couldn't help," Simon cried,

"and committees take way too much time to decide,

and the man with the book thinks it's good if we're through,

then what could this one little boy ever do?"

At first the young lad, for a minute or three,

just stared at the starfish stuck there by the sea,

then took a step forward and reached to the sand,

and he picked up a yellow starfish in his hand.

He stared at the creature, then gazed into space,

and a look of compassion swept over his face.

He cocked back his arm and he held the star tight,

then he hurled it forward with all of his might.

It flew from his hand and soared quickly away,

and then it splashed down and sank into the bay.

But the boy didn't stop—no, he kept right on going,

he kept right on grabbing and kept right on throwing

those starfish back into the sea from the shore,

and before long he'd saved 40 starfish or more.

The little old man—who'd been watching nearby—
asked, "What do you think that you're doing? And why?"
The boy answered, "Mister, these starfish won't last
if they don't get back into the water—and fast!"

The man shook his head and he chuckled a bit,

and said, "That's awfully sweet, but you might as well quit.

With thousands of starfish spread out on the beach,

this problem's solution is way beyond reach.

And nothing you do (it's quite sad but it's so)

could possibly make any difference, you know."

The boy paused a moment and turned to the man,
then showed him the starfish he held in his hand—
a small purple starfish left back by the tide—
and the youngster looked up at the man and replied,
"I really don't mean to be difficult, sir,
but it makes a big difference to this one, I'm sure."

With that Simon found himself launched to the sky—
saw the sand pass below—felt the air whistle by—
till he started to drop to the sea through the spray,
and landed—kersplash!—at last back in the bay.

So Simon was safe and the danger had ended
as slowly that small, purple starfish descended
down into the ocean and back to his home
underneath all the water, the surf, and the foam.
And Simon was saved, all his friends understood,
because one little boy had just done what he could.

70978676R00020

Made in the USA
San Bernardino, CA
09 March 2018